JUV/E
PS
595
.H35
G45
2003
CHINAT

Chicago Public Library

R0179623062

Halloween night : twenty-one spooktacula

P9-AQI-559

Chicago Public Library
Chinatown Branch
2353 S. Wentworth Avenue
Chicago, IL 60616
(312) 747-8013

9-03

**Halloween
Night**

Halloween Night

Twenty-one Spooktacular Poems

by Charles Ghigna

Illustrated by Adam McCauley

Running Press
KIDS
PHILADELPHIA • LONDON

Text © 2003 by Charles Ghigna
Illustrations © 2003 by Adam McCauley
All rights reserved under the Pan-American and International Copyright Conventions

Printed in China

This book may not be reproduced in whole or in part, in any form or by any means,
electronic or mechanical, including photocopying, recording, or by any information storage and retrieval system
now known or hereafter invented, without written permission from the publisher.

9   8   7   6   5   4   3   2   1
Digit on the right indicates the number of this printing

Library of Congress Control Number 2002095675

ISBN 0-7624-1552-5
Designed by Frances J. Soo Ping Chow
Acquired by Patty Aitken Smith
Edited by Patty Aitken Smith and Susan K. Hom
Typography: Ad lib ICG, Bell Gothic,
Mister Frisky, Uncle Stinky, and Willow

This book may be ordered by mail from the publisher.
Please include $2.50 for postage and handling.
But try your bookstore first!

Published by Running Press Kids,
an imprint of
Running Press Book Publishers
125 South Twenty-second Street
Philadelphia, Pennsylvania 19103-4399

Visit us on the web!
www.runningpress.com

R0179623062

For Chip and Julie

with a special thanks to Susan Hom, Patty Aitken Smith,
Frances Soo Ping Chow, Andra Serlin, Elizabeth Shiflett, and Jennifer Worick
for all their monstrous work on this boodacious book.

—C.G.

For Kevin

—A.M.

CONTENTS

My Secret List

Last year I made a secret list
Of houses on our street
That gave out all the very best
Of treats I like to eat.

I made a separate list of those
That gave out candy bars
And those that let us pick right from
Their giant candy jars.

I marked off all the houses that
Gave raisins in a box
And those that gave just one small piece
Of gum that's hard as rocks.

My little sister laughs at me,
But I don't think she's funny,
'Cause she won't let me see HER list—
Of houses that gave money!

What to Wear on Halloween?

Last year I went as Frankenstein,
The year before, a ghost.
This year I'd like to go as what
We kids all fear the most.

I've searched through stores all over town
For one old scary ghoul,
But none have masks that look just like
Our principal at school.

COSTUME CRAZY

The year I dressed up as a witch,
My ugly wig began to itch.

The year I dressed up as a clown,
My silly nose kept falling down.

The year I dressed up as a ghost,
I tripped and fell and hit a post.

This year I know just what I'll be.
I'm dressing up to go as me.

HaPpY HaLLoWeeN!

I'd rather be foolish than ghoulish,
I'd rather dress up as a clown;
I'd rather wear clothes with polka dot bows,
I'd much rather smile than frown.

I'd rather be kooky than spooky,
I'd rather be friendly than mean;
I'd rather go greeting than tricking and treating,
I'd rather have fun Halloween!

DEaR FrANkeNSTeiN

You walk stiff-legged like a man
Who came back from the dead.
You wear a bolt right through your neck
To hold your giant head.

I wonder if you'd like to look
The way we humans do.
Or do you think that we are cool
When we dress up like you?

My sister had to go with us
Last year to trick-or-treat.
My mom told me I had to wait
And help her cross the street.

She wore a little furry suit
With whiskers and a tail.
To carry all her treats she brought
An orange pumpkin pail.

She wouldn't let go of my hand.
She stayed right by my side.
Every time some kid yelled "Boo!"
She tried to run and hide.

My sister's scared of everything,
Especially at night.
Each time she saw her shadow,
She squeezed my hand real tight.

Her little kitten suit was cute.
I have to give her that.
But every time she tried to hide,
I called her "Scaredy-Cat!"

My Sister's Afraid of Halloween

The Candy Check

Parents say the candy check
Is something they must do.
They have to search for anything
That might be bad for you.

Although they never find a thing
Despite this careful chore,
It's funny how the bag comes back
Much lighter than before!

SLUMBER PARTY SURPRISE

We sat around the living room
And turned out every light,
Then started telling stories that
Would keep us up all night.

We passed around a flashlight as
We told our favorite tale;
The room was filled with shadows and
Each face grew gray and pale.

Then after every ghostly yarn
We searched around the room
To see if zombies hid within
The dark and dreary gloom.

We searched behind the sofa and
We checked beneath each chair
To make sure nothing drifted in
Upon the midnight air.

The longer that we stayed awake
The darker things became.
Our flashlight faded in the night
And closed our ghostly game.

A chilling hush fell over us
As right before our eyes
Appeared a most appalling sight
That caught us by surprise.

A shadow drifted down the stairs
Appearing pale and calm,
But when it shouted, "Go to bed!"
I knew it was my mom.

Beware
the Werewolf

Gray clouds creep across the sky,
The sun hides out of sight,
Something's crawling through the mist
And heading here tonight.

It's wailing through the wild woods,
It's peering through the trees,
It's coming after all of us
Upon an autumn breeze.

It wears a shroud of shadows,
It darkens every door,
It's on its way to your house now
And bringing gloom and gore.

Beware of where you're going,
Beware of where you play,
Beware of werewolves everywhere—
Halloween is on the way!

My Very Own MONSTER PET

I would like a monster pet,
The kind that children never get;
Something mean and extra large
That likes to bite or squeeze or charge:

A King Kong kind of chimpanzee,
A snake the size of Tennessee,
A two-ton kicking kangaroo,
A rhino bigger than a zoo,

A grizzly bear with sharpened claws,
A wild boar with giant jaws,
A porcupine with poison quills,
A tiger shark with razor gills,

An armadillo made of steel,
A nuclear electric eel!
That's what I wish that I could get,
A vicious, wild, monster pet.

But if I can't have one of these,
(No dogs, or cats, or goldfish, please);
I'll take the pet I most adore . . .

I'll settle for a dinosaur.

I'm Not Afraid

Thank you for the water
And the extra goodnight kiss.
I know it's getting late but first
I have to tell you this.

I'm not afraid of scary things
That dance out in the dark.
I'm not afraid of mournful sounds
That make the dogs all bark.

I'm not afraid of closet doors
When they are open wide.
I'm not afraid of drapes and shades
Where shadows like to hide.

I'm not afraid of ghosts and ghouls
That haunt each Halloween.
I'm not afraid of anything
That I have never seen.

I'm not afraid of creaking steps
Or gurgles in the sink.
I'm not afraid of basement groans
(At least that's what I think).

I'm not afraid of all those things
That bump or growl at night.
I'm not afraid of anything—
But please leave on the light.

PuMPKiN PAtcHeD

We drove out to the pumpkin patch
To see what we could find.
But soon we found that each of us
Had something else in mind.

My mom said, "Pick a shiny one
That's ripe and rather round,"
My dad said, "Pick the biggest one
That we have ever found."

My sister shouted, "Pick the one
That's fatter than the rest!"
But I knew if we looked around
We'd find which one was best.

We came upon a little one
That sat there all alone
Looking like she needed us
To please just take her home.

My parents said she was too small,
Her color was not right.
But when they saw me holding her,
They took her home that night.

They placed her on the table top
And asked us to decide
Who would cut the eyes and mouth
And who would scoop inside.

They handed me the carving knife,
But I just shook my head.
I couldn't bear to cut her up
No matter what they said.

And so she sits just as she was
Upon the windowsill.
Instead of Jack-o'-Lantern now
This year we have a Jill.

Pumpkins

ON GUARD

Look at all the pumpkin faces
Lighting up so many places.

On the porch and in the yard,
Pumpkin faces standing guard.

Looking friendly, looking mean,
With a smile or with a scream.

Orange faces burning bright
In the cool October night.

A GHOSTLY NIGHT

Cats and bats and witches' hats
The color of spilled ink,
Jack-o'-lanterns at each door,
I think I saw one wink!

Echoes bounce from house to house
In waves of "Trick or Treat"
As distant sounds of barking dogs
Come drifting down the street.

An owl questions who we are
These strangers in the night
All dressed up in eerie clothes
Beneath the pale moonlight.

A skeleton goes running by
Beside a fairy queen,
What is this happy, haunted night?
It must be Halloween!

Gargoyles

As still as stones they sit and stare
To scare you with their ghoulish glare.

If you should ever pass one by,
Do not look them in the eye.

Especially, for heaven sakes,
Beware the one whose hair is snakes!

The Two-Headed
Ghoul

It has two heads with four big feet.
It's coming down from up the street.

It has two mouths with four big ears.
There's nothing that it ever fears.

It laughs each time it calls our name.
We're caught inside its nightmare game.

It's getting close, don't make it mad.
Here it comes—it's Mom and Dad!

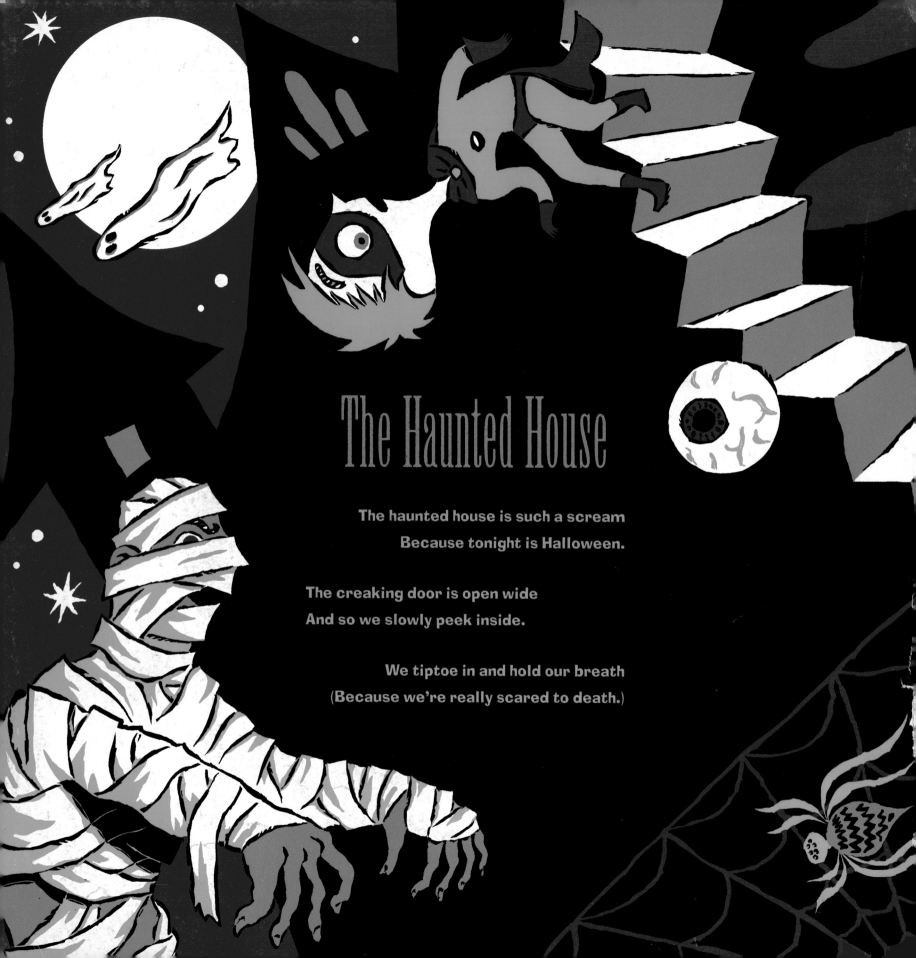

The Haunted House

The haunted house is such a scream
Because tonight is Halloween.

The creaking door is open wide
And so we slowly peek inside.

We tiptoe in and hold our breath
(Because we're really scared to death.)

Two mummies greet us at the door
(Or maybe three, or was it four?)

They lead us to the living room
Through smoky clouds of dewy doom,

Then down a hall where spiders spin
Three giant webs to catch us in.

Lost among the mournful maze
We wander through this haunted haze.

We climb some stairs into a place
Where eyes float by without a face.

And then a witch with eyes aglow
Grabs us as we start to go.

She holds us back and with a shout,
"I've got you now, there's no way out!"

We hear our hearts pound in our ears
While fighting back a flood of tears.

We break away and then we hide
And wish that we had stayed outside.

Then suddenly across the floor
A flash of light leads to a door.

A pumpkin shines its candlelight
And points the way back to the night.

Then once outside we start to grin—
'Cause now we want to go back in!

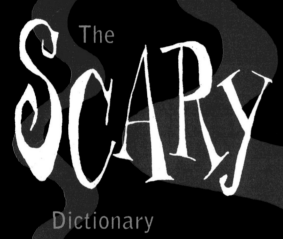

The **Scary** Dictionary

The biggest book you'll ever see
Hides deep inside the library.

It sits upon an antique stand
Waiting for your trembling hand.

Don't be afraid. Don't try to hide.
Just open it and look inside.

But watch out for those scary words
That jump at you like frightened birds.

Words like CRAWLY, CREEPY, CRUD
That make your thumping heart go thud.

Words like FEAR and FRANKENSTEIN
That send cold shivers up your spine.

Words like GHASTLY, GHOST, and GHOUL
That make your red-hot blood run cool.

Words like SCARY, SCREECH, and SCREAM
That give you nightmares when you dream.

Words like WEREWOLF, WARLOCK, and WITCH
That make your nerves begin to twitch.

Beware that awful burning need
To look inside and start to read.

'Cause every word that's mean and scary
Is found inside the dictionary!

It's Halloween!

It's Halloween
When witches scream,
When Owls hoo,
And Goblins boo.

It's trick-or-treat
Out in the street
When werewolves howl
And gargoyles growl.

It's time to scare
When monsters stare
And we all swear
There's nothing there!

Witch Way

With warts on her nose

And sharp pointy toes,

She flies through the night

on her broom.

With covers pulled tight

In the shadows of night,

I hide in the dark of my room.

SICK OR TREAT

I got a lot of treats tonight
And I just ate them all.
From candy bars to bubble gum,
My taste buds had a ball.

But now my stomach's doing flips.
Oh what a Halloween.
The biggest trick from all those treats?
I'm slowly turning green.